To Wyatt, Ryder, and Dusty,
my grandsons who inspire me
to reframe my childhood.

Dear Reader,

The differences between introverts and extroverts are surprising but seem rooted in the level of outside stimulation each needs to feel comfortable. Introverts prefer less stimulation while extroverts thrive on it. Consequently, introverts often opt for solitude.

Introverts are not necessarily shy but they may be. They are often quiet, thoughtful, and frequently dislike conflict. An introverted child might play by themselves at the park or move away from the group at a birthday party. Drive-throughs are often more comfortable than eating in a busy, noisy fast food restaurant. Even grocery stores with bright lights, intense odors, and crowds might undermine an introverted child's sense of wellbeing.

The young boy in *All By Myself* is intuitively taking care of himself by reducing the stimulation in his surroundings. The book is an invitation to parents, teachers, and especially children to acknowledge that all of us do not respond to stimulation in the same way. Introverted children are valuable, creative, reflective thinkers who deserve our empathy and respect. The world would be a very different place without the innumerable contributions of introverts.

-Karen Ann Leonard

All By Myself

Requests for permission to make copies of any part of the work should
be submitted online at info@mascotbooks.com or mailed to Mascot
Books, 560 Herndon Parkway #120, Herndon, VA 20170.

PRT0914A
Library of Congress Control Number: 2014913511

Printed in the United States

ISBN-13: 978-1-62086-939-0

www.mascotbooks.com

All By Myself

Karen Ann
Leonard

Illustrated By
Tamara Antonijevic

Sometimes I just want
to be all by myself.

When it's just me, it's wonderfully quiet.

I feel warm and safe, almost like I'm being held.

With no one else around, it's not noisy or loud.
I don't even think about covering my ears.

Quiet is so delicious.

All by myself isn't too bright or too scary.

It's calm, relaxing, and comfortable.

It's an indoor

or outdoor activity.

And it's up to you

whether it's lively

or restful.

Sometimes when I'm all by myself
my sister teases me.

She calls me goofy and weird.

I create all sorts of
wonderful imaginary things.

And amazing stories just pop into
my head.

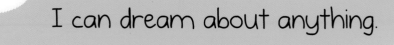

I can dream about anything.

Magic happens in my mind.

All by myself looks different every time.
I can sit down or lie down.

Twirling or headstands
are also options.

And there's always reading or counting. Endless possibilities.

Have you ever thought about being all by yourself?

It's really worth trying.

You might even like it. Not everyone likes it, but you won't know if you don't try.

One of the very best things about being all by yourself is that it's so easy to change. When you're finished being all by yourself, just walk up to someone and say hi.

Then, you're not
all by yourself
anymore.

I hope you like being all by yourself.

I sure do.

The END

This is Karen Ann Leonard's first book. She has experienced being a daughter, student, wife, mother, and grandmother through the eyes of an introvert. A graduate of Mount Holyoke College, she resides in the San Francisco Bay area in close proximity to her children and grandchildren.

Have a book idea?
Contact us at:

**Mascot Books
560 Herndon Parkway
Suite 120
Herndon, VA 20170**

info@mascotbooks.com | www.mascotbooks.com